Summer of the Cats

Illustrated by Karin Littlewood

Mark and Lucy love feeding the feral cats
at the deserted Hightop House. But when
the building is sold it soon becomes clear
that the cats need a new home – and fast!
But will they find one before it's too late?

Summer of the Cats

Ann Turnbull

A Magnet Book

First published in 1987
by Methuen Children's Books Ltd
This Magnet paperback edition first published 1988
by Methuen Children's Books Ltd
A Division of OPG Services Limited,
Michelin House, 81 Fulham Road, London SW3 6RB
Text copyright © 1987 Ann Turnbull
Illustrations copyright © 1987 Karin Littlewood
Printed in Great Britain by
Cox & Wyman Ltd, Reading

ISBN 0 416 08562 8

Contents

One 'What About the Cats?'

Ringtail heard the crunch of tyres on gravel.
She stood up, a protest rumbling in her
throat.

She had been dozing in the dusty peace of
the empty house. Her three kittens, sleepy
with milk, lay curled together, breathing
softly.

Outside, a car door slammed. Ringtail ad-
vanced into the hall, growling. Snowy was
there, her back arched.

Voices. Footsteps coming up the drive.

The kittens, sensing Ringtail's anxiety,

tumbled out of the den under the stairs and gathered round her, mewing.

Ringtail picked up a kitten in her teeth and Snowy took another. They hurried into the kitchen and out through the hole in the back door. Ringtail hid her kitten in the grass and ran back. She seized the last one in her teeth just as a key turned in the lock and the front door opened. Racing into the kitchen she plunged to safety through the hole and out into the wild green garden.

She dropped the kitten, and crouched beside Snowy in the long grass. The sun was warm. Insects buzzed, and the kittens batted at them. Ringtail's fear subsided. She stretched out, enjoying the sun. Her home had been invaded, but her kittens were safe. No one had seen them.

Ringtail was mistaken. Mark Easton had seen them. He put the binoculars down on the bedroom windowsill and ran downstairs.

'Mum!' he called. 'There are some people at Hightop House!'

In the kitchen his mother was darting from sink to cooker. She looked harassed.

'Can you lay the table, please, Mark?' she said. 'I'm all behind with the dinner, and Jane Rofe is picking me up at half-past two to play badminton.'

Mark rummaged unwillingly in the cutlery drawer.

'Ringtail and Snowy were scared,' he said. 'I saw them dash out and hide the kittens.'

'I told you I'd seen a car there, didn't I?' his mother said, turning down the heat under a fizzing pan. 'Jane thinks the house has been sold.'

'No one could live there,' said Mark. 'It's falling to bits.'

His mother laughed. 'Nothing much wrong with it! The roof's bad. But they'll do it up. Jane says it's going to be a bed and breakfast place – for the tourists. It's big enough. There must be six or eight bedrooms.'

Mark didn't care how many bedrooms there were.

'But what about the cats?' he asked.

The back door opened and his father came in, earthy from the vegetable patch.

'Dinner's ready,' said his mother. 'Mark, go and tell Lucy to come in and wash her hands.'

Mark went out. Lucy was in the front garden, pushing a doll's pram full of teddies at high speed across the lawn. It crashed into the rockery, scattering its occupants.

'They're in a rocket,' Lucy explained. 'They've landed on an alien planet.'

'Mum says wash your hands,' said Mark.

He went to the garden gate and looked across the road at the big house. The car – a green Citroen – was still there. He stared at it resentfully. What right had anyone got to buy Hightop House? It had been empty for years, the neighbours said. Except for the cats. 'Mark's cats,' his mother called them. But they weren't his. They weren't anyone's. They were wild.

His mother's voice came crossly: 'Mark! Hurry up!'

'Coming!' he called.

After dinner Jane Rofe arrived, full of gossip. Mark heard her ringing laughter in the hall and fled upstairs, lurking in his bedroom until she had gathered up his mother and the badminton racquets and whisked them away in her car.

The drive of Hightop House was empty.

Mark made himself wait an hour before going over there. He always fed the cats at ten to four on weekdays and he knew they would expect him at the same time at the weekend.

He opened a tin and tipped cat food on to two plates.

Lucy came into the kitchen.

'I'll come too.'

'All right,' said Mark. 'But don't try to grab the kittens. You frightened them yesterday.'

He gave her a plate to carry.

They walked carefully out to the road, pausing at the kerb as a lorry came banging under the bridge, then crossing over, into the open drive of Hightop House.

The house rose in front of them – old, shabby, with boarded-up windows and broken roof. They walked past a derelict barn and round the side of the house to the back door.

The cats were waiting: the pretty tabby, Ringtail, with the big eyes and series of dark rings encircling her tail; the other female, Snowy; and three toms – Big Tom, Whitepaws and Scarface.

The toms crowded around them. Scarface was the boldest – the crooked scar running from ear to nose proved him an adventurer. He pressed, purring, against Lucy's bare legs. Lucy laughed. 'He tickles!' The plate wobbled in her hands.

They set the plates down. The toms began to eat, but Mark and Lucy had to move back a few paces before Ringtail and Snowy would come near.

'Snowy's greedy,' said Lucy, as the females ate. 'Look how fat she's getting.'

'She's going to have kittens,' said Mark.

Lucy looked up at him and smiled,

delighted. Until today Mark had been pleased, too, but now he was not so sure it was good news.

'I hope she'll be all right,' he said.

Ringtail's kittens sniffed at the food, but did not eat. They were too young, and their mother's milk was enough.

Lucy sighed. 'I want to hold the kittens!'

'Ringtail will go for you.'

'I know.'

Lucy had overheard Jane Rofe and their mother talking about Hightop House. She said, 'Will the new people stop us coming in here?'

'They might', said Mark. He felt an anxiety that he couldn't express to Lucy. 'We'll just carry on feeding the cats until the people move in, anyway', he assured her confidently.

But his father had other ideas.

Two Cats in Danger

It was Sunday breakfast-time. Lucy was spreading honey and chattering.

'Tabby is naughty,' she said. 'He keeps running away and Ringtail has to fetch him back in her teeth. We've given them all names: Tabby, Patch, and Jet. Jet is jet-black all over; she's my favourite. Mark says Snowy is going to have kittens, too – '

'She's not, is she?' their father interrupted.

'Yes,' said Mark.

His father looked concerned. 'Mark – you know you've got to stop feeding the cats?'

Both children stared. 'Why?'

'The house has been sold.'

'But Mum said – '

'I didn't think it mattered,' said their mother. 'No one is living there yet. The children only go in the garden, and everyone uses the garden as a short cut to Lees Bank. You can see the track through the grass.'

'We can carry on feeding the cats until the builders move in, can't we?' said Mark. 'Mum said we could.'

'Those cats,' said his father, 'will all have to be cleared out, you know. No one's going to put up with that lot breeding all over the place.'

There was a moment's silence.

Mark knew what the answer would be, but he asked anyway: 'How will they clear them out?'

'I don't know. Pest Control.'

'But what will they do?'

'Trap them, probably.'

'But what will happen to them then?'

'They'll be put down,' his mother said.

'Killed?'

'Yes.'

Mark jumped up, rattling the table and knocking a sticky knife to the floor. 'But that's not fair! They're not doing any harm.'

'They could live somewhere else,' Lucy said.

Crazy ideas leapt into Mark's mind: 'We could find them another home . . . we could move them . . . only, they're so wild . . .'

'They might move of their own accord,' his mother said, 'if people keep coming and disturbing them.'

Mark saw hope. 'Do you think they will?'

'Not if you carry on feeding them', his father warned. 'You feed them, and they'll stay.'

Mark saw the sense of that. And yet how could he let them down? He felt his chin wobbling, and dived under the table to retrieve the fallen knife. From there he heard Lucy say, '*Please* can we feed them?'

Mark took out his dismay on Lucy: 'No!' he shouted, banging the knife back on to his plate. 'Dad's just told you why not!'

Lucy began to cry.

Their mother shot Mark a look of exasperation and began clearing the table.

Their father lifted Lucy up and began explaining the problem all over again.

'We can go and watch them, though, can't we?' Mark pleaded.

Mr Easton sighed, and looked at his wife's retreating back. 'I don't want you to get too attached to them.'

'But can we?' Mark persisted.

'I suppose so. Until someone comes.'

'It's all right, Lucy. We can still go and watch them,' Mark said. 'Shall we go over there now?'

Lucy nodded, wet-faced, and slid off her father's knee.

'I wanted to feed them', she muttered obstinately as she followed Mark out to the hall.

Mark was thinking about what his mother had said: the cats might move away. But where to? And how could he persuade them?

'Mark,' said Lucy in a tearful voice. 'Why can't we feed the cats?'

Mark produced an exaggerated sigh and ignored the question. It was bad enough trying to explain things to Lucy, let alone to a cat.

'Dad?' he called. 'If people want to buy a house, how long does it take?'

'Oh – ages,' his father said vaguely.

'How many days?'

'Not days. Weeks. Maybe months. They'd probably have to get a mortgage and they might have to sell their own house. Things can go wrong.'

'Oh, good,' said Mark softly. 'I hope they do.'

Perhaps nothing would happen for months. Perhaps never.

Lucy had fetched the binoculars from Mark's bedroom.

'We won't need those,' said Mark.

'I like them.'

'Let me carry them, then.'

They ran up the road and into the far end of the garden through the gap in the wall. Mark knew they could watch the cats from here without alarming them.

As they crept in amongst the long grass under the ash tree, Lucy said, 'Mark, will the cats starve if we don't feed them?'

'No.' Mark was confident. 'They're feral cats. That means they're wild animals. They don't need people.'

'What will they eat?'

'Mice. Birds. Perhaps frogs.'

Lucy pulled a face. 'They might like cat food better.'

'Look!' said Mark. 'Big Tom!'

The back wall of the barn was broken, and Big Tom had emerged from one of the gaps. He was a black and not-very-white cat with a broad, battle-scarred face. He settled down with his front paws curled under his chest and surveyed his territory.

Scarface followed him out, stretching his length on a patch of sunny wall.

The children waited. The cats sat.

Lucy sighed. 'It's boring without the kittens.'

'Go home, then.'

'No!'

'Well, if you're bored . . .'

'I'm only a little bit bored. Can I look through the binoculars?'

Mark handed them over.

Lucy focused on the distant wooded dale. A train went by on the viaduct, and she watched the laden goods wagons clattering past. The cats acknowledged the train with merely the slightest shift of ear angle, but as its sound receded, both of them were suddenly alert, heads turning towards the drive.

The green Citroen was back. It stopped at

the top of the drive, and two people got out: a tall bearded man and a fair-haired woman in jeans. The woman opened a handbag and brought out keys. Mark saw a movement by the back door: Ringtail and Snowy coming out with kittens in their mouths.

'Mark!' Lucy whispered. 'Are they going to live in the house?'

'Ssh! Get down!'

They crouched lower into the grass.

The woman put the key in the lock, and the couple went inside and shut the door. Mark and Lucy got up.

'We'd better go,' Mark said.

They slipped out through the gap in the wall. Mark turned back and looked anxiously towards the house.

'I hope those people don't see the cats,' he said. 'They look as if they might not like cats.'

They went home. The green Citroen stayed at Hightop House for an hour. Lucy lost interest and began riding around the garden on her bike, but Mark went up to his bedroom and watched until the couple got into their car and drove away. Then he went back alone to the house.

As he reached the garden Ringtail came out through the hole in the back door. She moved about restlessly, calling. She jumped back through the hole, then out again, then back in. She was obviously distressed.

Mark went closer. Jet and Patch were there, half-hidden amongst the nettles. They shrank away from him. He noticed that Tabby was not about. Was that why Ringtail was behaving so strangely? Had something happened to Tabby?

Three Mark Trespasses

Ringtail came out again, still calling. She saw Mark and flattened her ears, backing against the wall.

'It's all right, Ringtail,' said Mark. 'I won't hurt you. Have you lost Tabby?'

He tried to make his voice reassuring, but Ringtail hissed and arched her back.

Mark squatted and peered through the hole. He saw an uneven floor of red stone tiles, a strip of skirting-board, a half-open door and darkness beyond it.

As he drew back Ringtail rushed past him

22

and dived through the hole again. Mark looked in and watched her run to the half-open door and stand there, calling. And now he thought he heard something else: a high faint 'miaow' from inside the house. Tabby! He was hurt or trapped, and Ringtail couldn't reach him!

Ringtail disappeared from view. But a few seconds later she was back, hissing when she saw Mark's face at the hole. Mark retreated so that she could jump out. She ran to Jet and Patch and licked them briefly, as if afraid that Mark might have contaminated them.

Why couldn't she get Tabby out? Perhaps he was injured. How long would it be before anyone came here again? Days? Weeks? Tabby could die.

He pushed at the door. Locked. The hole was too small for him, but if he could make it bigger . . . He tested the wood above the hole; it was soft and rotting. He pressed harder. A piece of wood broke with a loud splintering crack. Ringtail picked up Jet and ran.

Mark looked around guiltily. The windows of the surrounding houses had become eyes, watching him. He had never done anything like this before. It seemed wrong, and yet the kitten had to be rescued.

He put his weight against the wood again,

forcing it inwards and upwards. It snapped and splintered, grazing his hand. He glanced around, expecting the entire neighbourhood to come running, but no one had heard. Ringtail and the kittens had fled.

The hole was big enough now. After another quick glance towards the road, he squeezed through it.

He looked around the room, seeing an old coal-fired cooker thick with dust and cobwebs, a shallow stone sink, and a wooden draining board. Cat footprints on the draining board led to a windowsill where a mat of hairs revealed a cat's favourite sitting place.

He heard more clearly now the tiny mewing of the kitten. But where was it coming from? He went through the doorway into a dim, dusty hall. A coloured glass fanlight in the front door threw a pattern of red and blue shapes on to the floorboards. Stairs led up into even darker places. Mark shivered. It was creepy.

He went past the front door and into a big room with plaster mouldings on its high ceiling. Next door was a smaller room with corner cupboards. The mewing persisted. It was near – but where? He opened the cupboard doors. There was nothing inside but mouse droppings and spiders' eggs.

He went back to the hall.

'Where are you?' he asked the persistent little cry.

As if in answer he heard a woman's loud voice. He jumped with fright. Someone was coming in! The new owners! And he was a trespasser – or was it a vandal? Or both?

He darted back to the kitchen – and ducked just in time as a woman passed the window, talking, apparently to a child below the level of the sill. Mark's panic slowed. It was Jane Rofe and Paula, taking the short cut to Lees Bank. But the banging of his heart had hardly subsided before he remembered the enlarged hole in the door and the broken wood scattered around. Jane must have noticed it – and she was bound to tell his mother. Would his mother guess he had done it?

He crouched on the kitchen floor until Jane and Paula had gone. Then he went back to the hall – and saw, for the first time, the door to a cupboard under the stairs. Mewing sounded behind it.

He opened the door. Tabby shot out, just as Ringtail dived into the kitchen again. She seized Tabby in her teeth and jumped out through the hole.

Mark realised that the man and woman

must have accidentally shut Tabby in the cupboard.

Climbing out through the broken door he stared guiltily at the smashed-up wood. Best to get away. He ran home fast.

That afternoon their parents allowed the children to feed the cats 'one last time'.

The next day, after school, Mark got a half-empty tin of cat food out of the fridge and showed it to his mother.

'It seems a waste. Couldn't I use it up?'

She hesitated. 'You'd better not. Just throw it away.'

'The cats will be there, waiting,' Mark said. His voice was choked.

'I know,' she said. 'I'm sorry.'

Mark stood with his head down, unable to speak.

'I saw a man there this morning,' his mother went on. 'Looked like a builder. They might start work on the place soon.'

Mark went out to the yard and dropped the tin into the dustbin.

'Mark?' said his mother.

'Yes?'

'Maybe we should have a pet cat?'

Mark banged the dustbin lid down. 'I don't want one!' he said angrily.

Four Trev

Ringtail and Snowy and the kittens cowered, terrified, in the barn.

Banging vibrated on the air and outraged their delicate eardrums.

There seemed to be men everywhere. They heard shouting and whistling, footsteps going backwards and forwards past the doorway. Near the house a black box blared out alarming sounds.

The two cats had moved into the barn when the house became unsafe, but Ringtail knew that they must get right away.

Whitepaws had already gone and Big Tom was restless.

Snowy mewed. Her kittens would soon be born and she felt uncomfortable. She had made a den near a pile of bricks, plucking at the ground and turning round and round until the space was her own.

Ringtail licked Snowy's head and sniffed at her own kittens. An urgent need arose in her to find a safer place for them all.

She slipped out of the barn and trotted across the garden and through a gap in the fence into the woodland. She was hunting – not for food, but for a new home.

Mark and Lucy ran across the road and into the drive of Hightop House.

The doorway of the barn was just inside the drive, on their right. The children knew that Snowy was about to have her kittens, and for several days they had been slipping in and out of the barn to see her without the builders noticing them.

They went in. The barn was dark and cool. A broken wall divided it in half, and the den was on the far side.

They saw Ringtail's kittens first.

'Ringtail's not here.' Mark was surprised.

Jet was studying a beetle, Patch pouncing

on an imaginary mouse. High above, Tabby balanced carefully along a beam.

Mark looked round for Snowy; there she was, in her den, and something else was moving there! He went closer. Lucy followed him.

'She's had them!' she whispered ecstatically.

They both stared.

Snowy lay on her side, and a heap of tiny squirming kittens jostled for her teats — three, four, maybe five of them; they could not go near enough to count.

Mark hardly dared to breathe in case he should frighten her.

'We'd better go,' he whispered.

Lucy nodded.

They crept outside.

As they stood blinking in the sunlight, one of the builders came out of the front door of the house, saw them, and approached.

It was too late to run.

'What are you doing here?' he called.

'Nothing,' said Mark.

The man towered over him. Mark, his head low, saw dusty blue jeans and a pair of huge shoes, the heavy-duty sort with steel toe caps. He studied the shoes while the inevitable lecture began.

'You shouldn't play here,' the man said. 'Dangerous. Do you come from the cottages?'

'Yes,' muttered Mark, trying to edge away.

'Which one?'

'Number one,' said Lucy brightly. She pointed. Mark scowled at her. Now the man would complain to their parents.

'You've not been there long, then?' the man said amiably. 'Used to be Lloyds lived there. Thirty years.'

Mark looked up, astonished.

'Thirty years in one house!'

'We've moved twice,' said Lucy. 'Mark remembers both times but I only remember one because I was eight months the first time.'

The man smiled. Mark felt less threatened. The builder was a big man, fair-haired and tanned, about the same age as their father but with a slow way of talking that made him sound older.

'I live up the Bank,' the man was saying. He jerked his head in the direction of Lees Bank. 'Lived there all my life. This place was a farm when I was little. We used to play in the fields.'

Lucy said, 'We came to see if Snowy had had her kittens, and she has.'

Mark's heart sank. Why did she have to mention the cats?

But the man, it seemed, knew all about them. 'Oh, you're after the cats, are you? Are they in there?'

'Snowy and the kittens are,' said Lucy. 'But Ringtail's away. And the toms.'

'So another one has had kittens, then? Can I see?'

He went into the barn.

Mark turned furiously on Lucy.

'Why did you tell him about the cats? Do you want them to be trapped?'

'I didn't know – ' Lucy began. Then the man came back, shaking his head.

'That'll clinch it,' he said. 'More kittens! You know they're going to clear them out?'

'When?' Mark asked desperately.

'I don't know when. But Mrs Fletcher – that's the lady that's bought the house – said they'd been on to a pest control firm about it. Well, you can't blame them. The place is over-run with cats. There must be dozens of them.'

'There are only five,' said Mark.

'And the kittens,' said Lucy.

'I'm sure I've seen more than five. I came in the back door the other day and nearly trod on a pile of them running along with kittens in their mouths.'

'How do they kill them?' Mark asked.

'Mrs Fletcher says this firm gasses them – chloroform. Well, it's quick; they don't feel anything, you know,' he added, seeing the children's horrified faces.

Mark said, 'But why can't they find homes for them?'

'You ever tried finding homes for kittens? Not enough homes to go round. Anyway, they're wild. My mate, Dave, he reckoned he was going to get one of the kittens for his little lad. He picks up this black one – you should have seen how it bit and scratched. He had to drop it.'

'That must have been Jet,' said Lucy.

The man smiled, sympathetically.

'You know them all, don't you?'

The children nodded, tears in their eyes.

'It's a quick death. And perhaps it's better for a wild thing than being caged up in one of these sanctuary places.'

'I suppose so,' Mark said forlornly.

Lucy said, 'Mummy thought they might find themselves a new home, but they haven't.'

'Well, they might yet. They seem to have left the house. Can't say I blame them, either; I'd leave it myself if I was a cat. And things are going to get noisier.'

A voice shouted from the house: 'Trev! What are you doing?'

'Coming!' the man shouted back.

He turned to the children. 'I've got to go. Now listen: you'd better keep away from here now. We can't have children running around the site – it's dangerous. Whatever happens about the cats, I'll come over and let you know, shall I?'

'Yes,' said Mark, and added, 'Thanks.'

Trev turned back to the house.

The children peeped once more into the barn before they left. A small persistent mewing came from high up: Tabby was trapped on the beam and couldn't get down.

Instinctively Mark went to help him.

'Tabby, you're always in trouble,' he said.

The beam was high, but he could reach it by climbing on the wall. He stretched out to touch the kitten, but Tabby backed away, hissing in tiny fright. Snowy was alert now, glaring at Mark.

Mark knew he was wasting his time. He climbed down. He'd have to leave it to Snowy.

Snowy, guarding her kittens, watched him with fierce eyes. And suddenly Mark felt furious with everyone: with Mrs Fletcher and the trappers who were planning to kill Snowy and her kittens, with Trev for talking soothingly of a quick death, and even with Snowy for not understanding the danger she was in.

He shouted at Snowy: 'You can't stay here! They're going to kill you!'

Snowy's ears went back. She hissed.

Mark turned to Lucy. 'We've got to save them,' he said. 'I'll think of a way. I won't let them be killed.'

Five Ringtail Goes Hunting

That night, as the midsummer dusk was falling, Ringtail sprang from the garden wall up and over the side of the railway bridge.

She had been searching for hours. First she had gone into the woodland, following the stream as it trickled through wet meadows. The woodland was good for hunting; she caught a mouse and a fledgling bird. But there was no shelter, nowhere to make a den.

She followed the stream back to the lake, climbed up to Lees Bank, and explored the gardens on the far side. Here there were sheds and garages, a pool to drink from, and even, in one garden, a pigeon loft full of fluttering birds. She stalked eagerly around it until a woman came out and flapped a cloth at her. But not only were there people, there were too many other cats, each with its own small territory. They crouched on walls and on footpaths, glaring at her until she backed away.

Now, she paused on the edge of the railway. The lines stretched into the distance in both directions. She turned towards the wooded dale.

She had not been going long before she reached the edge of her familiar hunting range. She had never ventured further than this point before. Woods rose on one side and factory buildings lay below on the other. She continued, all her senses alert.

There was a broken sapling by the side of the line, gleaming white where the wood had been snapped and torn off. Ringtail paused and sniffed all around it. It smelt of Big Tom. The scent reassured her, and she trotted on.

She had passed the factory now, and woodland crowded thickly on either side of the track. The air was dark. Her ears pricked at the rustle of roosting birds. An owl hoo-hooed high up in the trees. Night came on,

37

clear and bright with stars. The moon was full.

The woods began to thin on one side. She was coming into a clearing. A building loomed up. She stopped, and listened.

There was no unusual sound, so she approached the building cautiously. It was like the big house, but much more open. Doors and windows were missing.

She jumped up on the broken wall and went inside. Her paws encountered a wooden floor – rotting, old, smelling of damp and decay. Patches of sky showed through holes in the roof.

She passed through a doorway into another room. Here the roof was intact and the floorboards less broken, and there was a space, enclosed by brick walls, that smelt of soot. Ringtail crawled into it. It was cat-sized and cosy, and made her think of her kittens and the den at the big house. She scratched the floorboards to show her sense of belonging.

A doorway led into yet another room. She went through. It was similar to the last one, but there was also a broken floor with a space under it big enough to crawl into, and a pile of bricks in one corner with a hidey-hole behind them.

She came out into the clearing. There she found cinders and broken bricks and a sooty place where a fire had been. A rusty oil drum lay on its side. Warily, Ringtail crept into it. The drum wobbled, and she braced herself, feet wide apart. She settled down and looked out. It was good; a bolt-hole, a place to hide if danger threatened.

Behind it were the woods. She came out of the oil drum and pushed in amongst ash and elder and strong-smelling wild garlic.

She came to a ditch – a trickle of water with gnats hanging over it.

She crouched, listening. Birds rustled, too high. A car droned by on the road above. Something squeaked. Her ears swivelled to the sound. It came again. She lay low, ears forward, tail beginning to twitch.

A rustle betrayed her prey.

She pounced, and caught the mouse between her front paws. She tossed it, took it in her mouth, dropped it – draggled and dazed – and let it run a little, pounced again and batted it between her paws until it was stunned. Then she killed it with a bite to the neck, bit off its head, and ate the mouse hungrily, leaving only the intestines.

She sat up, cleaned her face and paws with delicate care, and went back to the clearing.

Ringtail was satisfied. She trotted off down the railway line without hesitation, all nervousness gone, intent on fetching the kittens. She sniffed at the scent markers along the way, and made new marks of her own. They would reassure Snowy, and the toms might find them if they came this way.

She passed the factory, crossed the road and the lake, and reached the place where the familiar shape of the big house rose on the skyline.

She sprang down on to the garden wall and ran along it until she came to the barn.

Snowy was there, in the doorway, upright and tense, with wide eyes; Jet and Patch were beside her. As soon as she saw them Ringtail felt her fur prickle and rise; she sensed with her whole being that something was terribly wrong.

Six Trapped!

Mark could not sleep. He was allowed to stay up later at this time of year because the evenings were light, but still he lay awake.

Car sounds and voices in the street outside were loud and disturbing. He got up and went to the window.

A group of teenagers was going by, pushing and shoving each other, the girls shrieking with laughter. The bridge, silhouetted against the rosy after-glow, made their voices echo as they went underneath. Mark stared, squinting: something was moving on top of the bridge. A cat! It had jumped up from the wall of Hightop House, paused on the parapet, then dropped down on to the line. He had not seen which one it was. He stared along the railway line, wondering where it was going; hunting, he supposed.

Wide awake now, he padded out to the bathroom and got a drink of water. The vinyl tiled floor cooled his bare feet. When he came out he could hear the gentle regular sound of Lucy's breathing coming from the next room.

He got back into bed, turned his pillow over to find the cooler underside, thumped it, flopped down, and lay spreadeagled.

He must have dozed, because when he woke again it was quite dark, the burbling of the television had stopped, and there were no more voices in the street. He was sweaty. The bed was hot and prickly and there seemed to be no cool spaces left. He groped for his watch and switched on its tiny light: twelve forty-seven.

Mark had never been awake so late before. He wondered if the cat had come back. He got up and went to the window.

A dark-coloured van was parked in the drive of Hightop House. Its rear was towards him and he could not see if there was any name on the side. It was not the builder's van; that was light blue. Who could it be? Who would come to Hightop House at twelve forty-seven at night?

Suddenly he knew. The shock washed over him, momentarily paralysing. Then he dashed from the room out on to the landing.

The stairwell was dark. His parents had gone to bed.

He paused, clenching and unclenching his fists.

Should he wake them? By the time they were up it would be too late. There was no one to turn to.

He ran back to the window. The van was still there, but no light showed in the house or the barn. Nothing moved. Where would the trapper be? In the barn, probably. Mrs Fletcher would have told him that the cats were now living there. He imagined the trapper in the dark barn, moving softly so as not to frighten the cats, setting up his deadly bait . . .

Mark knew he had to go over there. He didn't think about what he could do, only that he had to be there. He couldn't let the cats be taken while he stood watching from his bedroom window.

He went back on to the landing and began creeping down the stairs.

He found his shoes in the hall, and shoved his feet into them without undoing the laces.

Carefully he opened the front door and pushed the knob down on the Yale lock so that it could not spring shut. He stepped outside and closed the door behind him.

The night breeze was mild and fresh after the hot bedroom. He crept down the path, glancing back furtively at the house, even though his parents slept at the back and would not be able to hear him now.

He heard footsteps and voices approaching, and ducked quickly behind the gate as two men came along the road, walking briskly, their footsteps ringing in the empty street. Mark waited until they had passed by. Then he gently unlatched the gate, closed it, and darted across the road.

He paused in the entrance to Hightop House drive. He was only yards from the van. The rear doors were open. It was empty. He listened. No sound came from the barn.

He could see the black doorway of the barn just a few yards away, but he dared not go in: the trapper might be there. Now that he was outside he did not know what to do. He remembered the other way in, through the end of the garden. He could see into the barn from there without being seen.

He ran up the road and into the garden through the gap in the wall, then picked his

45

way cautiously through grass and nettles towards the broken wall of the barn.

He climbed up and peered in. Darkness. No movement. The bright moonlight did not penetrate here and his eyes were not yet accustomed to the dark. Gradually, as he watched, he began to make out familiar shapes: the beams, the pile of bricks where Snowy had her den. There was the white blur that must be Snowy, curled up there with her kittens. He became aware of the wall that divided up the inside of the barn.

The entrance to the barn was out of sight behind the interior wall. Was the trapper hiding behind the wall? Mark's heart had been pounding fearfully as he approached the barn, but now it seemed so quiet and unchanged that he began to wonder if he had been mistaken. The van was there, but he had no proof that it was the trapper's van.

He began to feel silly, crouching there in his pyjamas in the middle of the night. Even the cats did not seem to be about. Was the one he had seen on the railway line still out?

He jumped when something moved in the shadows. But it was only Scarface. The white cat sprang down from a beam and began to pad purposefully towards the other side of the wall.

He paused once, and lifted his head, as if to catch a scent. He went round the corner.

And suddenly Mark saw it: the edge of the cage projecting beyond the wall.

He leapt down into the barn, landing painfully on sharp rubble.

'No!' he yelled.

But he was too late.

He heard the trap bang shut, the terrified yowling of Scarface and the crash of his body against the wire mesh side. Snowy stood up, hissing fearfully.

Mark dashed across the barn. Scarface was hurling himself against the sides of the cage in a frenzy of terror. His lips were drawn back and his eyes crazed. The cage shook with the weight of his fear. Blood spurted on his face and flecks of blood spattered across his white fur.

Mark could not bear it.

'Stop!' he screamed. 'Scarface! Stop! Stop!'

And then he looked up into the startled face of the trapper.

It was a woman: a rough-looking woman in jeans and donkey jacket with her hair tied back in a pony-tail.

She swore under her breath.

'A kid!' she exclaimed. 'You gave me such a fright! What the hell are you doing here?'

'Let him go!' Mark begged. 'Please, please, let him go.'

'No way!' the woman said, shouting to make herself heard above the cat's yowling and crashing. 'I don't get paid to let him go. You run off home. You shouldn't be out here. Where're you from?'

Dumbly Mark pointed to the cottages.

'Well, get back there. Go on!'

She heaved up the cage with the frenzied cat still beating against the sides and walked out to the van. Mark heard the cage bang on to the metal floor and the doors slam shut.

He dashed out. The woman was getting into the driver's seat.

'Get home!' she said again as the engine came to life.

She drove up to the house, turned round, and began to ease the van carefully out on to the road.

'Where are you taking him?' Mark yelled.

No answer. The van moved out and off down the road. Mark heard Scarface howling as the van sped under the bridge, and then the sound of the engine dwindled into the distance and faded away.

For a moment Mark was too stunned to move. Then he dashed across the road, up the garden path and into his house.

He ran up the stairs shouting, 'Mum! Dad! Quick! They've taken Scarface!'

The landing light came on. He stood blinking. His mother had staggered sleepily out.

'What on – Mark!' she screamed. 'What have
you done? You're all covered in blood! What's
happened? Where – '

His father appeared behind her, and everyone began shouting at once.

Mark saw that his pyjama trousers were
torn, that his knee was bleeding, he had
scraped his elbow, and was covered in dirt
from the barn.

He flopped down on the landing and began
to cry.

Seven A Lost Kitten

Ringtail was afraid when she entered the barn. Its atmosphere spoke to her: fear, it said; blood; danger; run! She backed away from it and went outside and rubbed her body against Snowy's for comfort. But Snowy was tense; Ringtail could smell her fear. She knew they had to get away.

She called her kittens. Jet and Patch came quickly, mewing and winding round their mother. Ringtail called again. No Tabby. She ran about, calling and searching, but he was not to be found. Ringtail was distressed, but the instinct to get Jet and Patch away from the bad place was stronger than her need to find Tabby. She would come back for him.

Snowy ran into the barn and picked up one of her kittens in her teeth. Ringtail followed her and picked up another. She went straight to the garden wall, and up on to the bridge. Jet and Patch followed her, but Snowy ran off into the undergrowth in the back garden, desperate to hide her kitten. She was distracted. All night she had been moving her kittens around the barn from one hidey-hole to another, and then back to the den. She dropped the kitten into the grass under the ash tree, went halfway back to the barn, then returned, and picked it up again.

It was some time after Ringtail had disappeared over the side of the bridge that Snowy turned in the same direction. She smelt Ringtail's scent on the wall next to the bridge. Comforted, she jumped up and followed in Ringtail's track.

Back at Hightop House, all that was left of the cat colony was a nest of three newborn kittens in the barn and, somewhere, the missing Tabby.

By sunrise Snowy and Ringtail had been back to the barn and removed two more kittens, but although Ringtail called – the special chirruping call she used for her kittens – there was no answering mew from Tabby.

At about eight in the morning the builder's van turned into the drive of Hightop House. The day was already heating up. At half-past eight Mark and Lucy stood at the entrance to the drive, shouting, 'Trev! Trev!'

Trev was outside, near the back door, but there was a cement mixer churning away and so much banging from inside the house that he did not hear them.

They took a few steps up the drive, afraid to go in because they had been told not to.

'TREV!' they yelled in unison.

Trev heard them and came over.

Both children began gabbling at once. Mark was unable to continue and stood shaking with suppressed sobs. Trev was appalled.

'What is it? What's the matter?'

'Scarface – ' sobbed Lucy.

'Scarface,' said Mark, gulping for breath. 'Trapped. The trapper. Last night.'

'Took him away,' said Lucy.

'How do you know?' Trev asked.

Mark caught his breath. 'I saw. I came over and saw.'

He felt tears welling up, and smeared a dirty hand across his face.

'Now look – listen – you mustn't take on like this . . .'

Trev, upset himself, looked around helplessly. With an effort, Mark got his tears under control.

'Do you know who the trappers are? Can we phone them? Can we save him?' he pleaded.

Trev sighed and shook his head.

'It wouldn't do any good, Mark, even if I knew, which I don't, not without asking the Fletchers. He'll be gone by now. They chloroform them. It's quick. He'll have been done.'

'That's what Mummy and Daddy said.' Lucy's eyes were red.

'It was awful,' said Mark, his voice shaking, 'seeing him in the cage. He went crazy.'

'Well, that's it,' said Trev. 'They'll have put him down by now. They wouldn't leave him in that state, would they? It'd be too cruel.'

'She *was* cruel,' said Mark violently. 'I hated her. She didn't care.'

'It's just a job,' Trev said. 'Got to be done.'

'But she'll be back. She'll get the rest of them. They've got to get away.'

Trev sighed. 'They haven't gone yet,

anyway, that's for sure. The boss found a kitten in the cement mixer this morning.'

'Dead?' Mark was horrified.

'No, no. Just exploring. We hadn't switched on. Could have, though. The boss was none too pleased. Can't stand cats, John can't.'

'Where is it now?' Mark asked.

'Don't know. John threw it out with a few choice words. We haven't seen it since.'

Mark was still thinking of Scarface.

'Couldn't you ask those people for the phone number?' he persisted. 'He might not be dead yet.'

Trev put a hand on his shoulder.

'Mark, what would you do if they gave him back?'

'We could keep him at our house.'

'And all the others?'

Mark's lower lip quivered.

'I just don't want them to die!'

'Come on, now,' said Trev. 'I've got to get back to work and you'd better get home. You know I'd help if I could.'

Mark sniffed.

'Can we have a look in the barn and see if the others are there?'

Trev glanced towards the house. 'All right, but be quick. I don't want John to see you.

Like I said, he can't stand cats, and he aren't too bothered about children, neither.'

He turned to go to his work, then stopped and looked back.

'If I see any cats I'll let you know. I *am* sorry about Scarface.'

Mark nodded. They went into the barn. It seemed empty. Lucy ran to Snowy's den.

'Mark! There's just one kitten here!'

Mark came to see. The kitten, tiny and helpless, with sealed eyes, tottered to its feet and mewed.

Lucy put out a finger and touched its head.

'She's forgotten it. Poor little thing! Let's take it home.'

'No,' said Mark. 'Lucy! Perhaps they *are* moving away!'

'But why has she left this one?'

'She couldn't carry them all at once, could she?'

'I want to keep it,' Lucy said longingly.

'It would die. It needs its mother. Leave it. She'll come back. We'd better go, before John finds us.'

They scuttled out of the barn and across the road to their own house.

It was a Saturday. The heat made everyone tired. Their father, hoeing in the vegetable patch behind the house, was red-faced and shirtless. Their mother staggered into the garden with a basket of washing.

'After I've pegged this lot out,' she said, 'I'm going to collapse for the rest of the day.'

'Can we have the sprinkler on?' Lucy asked.

'No. It'll wet the washing.'

'The paddling pool, then?'

'Okay. Ask your dad.'

Lucy ran off.

Mark turned towards the house.

'You're not going indoors?' his mother demanded.

'It's too hot.'

She looked at him anxiously, trying to work out how he was feeling. Mark turned his face away.

'Mark?' she said. 'You're all right, are you?'

He nodded. 'Just hot,' he said, and escaped inside.

The binoculars were lying on the bedroom windowsill. He picked them up and focused on Hightop House.

He ranged all around the garden, seeing into the depths of the grass and nettles, watching two white butterflies fluttering, a dragonfly zigzagging towards the lake. The cats seemed to have gone.

He slid the binoculars down, to the heat

haze shimmering on the road, then into his own front garden. Shrieks of laughter came from the paddling pool. Lucy was in there with Gavin, the four year old from next door. Mark's father was flopped in a deck-chair under the laburnum. His mother, wearing a bikini, was stretched out on a rug in the sun.

He flicked across to the drive of Hightop House and focused on the churning cement mixer. Trev stood beside it, with a short

fair-haired man, mixing something in a bucket.

There was a strange van parked near by. The back doors were open, and Mark could see planks of wood inside. Near the front wheel something moved. A kitten. Tabby!

Tabby sniffed around the wheel, then came to the open back doors and sat poised, looking up. Mark could see that he was gauging the height for a spring. The next moment he was inside the van. He balanced along a plank, disappearing into the interior.

A man came out of the house. He walked briskly to the van, slammed the back doors shut, waved, and got into the driver's seat.

Mark flung down the binoculars in panic. The van was beginning to move. He raced out of his room, down the stairs, out of the front door, down the path, and threw himself against the gate. The van was moving off towards the bridge.

Mark waved frantically. 'Stop!' he shouted.

The driver waved back in a friendly way and drove off under the bridge.

Eight Tabby in Trouble

The van with Tabby in the back was on its way to Naylor's Woodyard at Liston, three miles away.

Tabby was frightened when the van began to move. The planks of wood bumped and banged and clattered and the van threw him against its hard metal sides. Tabby wanted to be back in the barn. And where was his mother? He mewed for her, but she did not come.

Barry Naylor, in the driver's seat, could not hear Tabby's tiny cries. Nor did he take much notice of the red Renault that had followed him all the way to Liston until it turned into the entrance to the woodyard behind him.

Barry stopped the van, jumped out, and went to the back doors just as the red car pulled up behind him. He opened the doors. From the red car people leapt out, shouting – men, children, all shouting and pointing. Barry recognised one of them, with surprise, as Trevor Jones. At that moment something shot out of the van, darted across the yard, and disappeared into a huge stack of planks. The children shrieked and shot after it.

'Trev,' said Barry, 'what on earth's going on?'

While Trev began explaining, Mark and Lucy squatted down and peered into the darkness at the back of the woodstack where Tabby had vanished. Nothing moved there.

Their father came up behind them.

'Any luck?'

'No. He's gone.'

'You know, he may not come out while we are all here. We might have to leave him,' their father said.

'But we can't leave him!' Mark protested. 'He needs Ringtail.'

'He'd probably find her again. Cats are not as helpless as you think.'

By this time Trev and Barry and two of Barry's workmates were there beside the woodstack, all offering ideas or shaking their heads.

Lucy was not interested in what the adults had to say; she was watching the stack.

She saw a small head emerge from between two rows of planks and peer cautiously around.

'He's there!' she whispered, nudging Mark.

'Dad!' Mark whispered. 'Lucy's seen him!'

They crept towards the place. Mark was nearest. He reached out gently, but his hand threw a shadow; the kitten saw it and darted back.

There was a gap between the two stacks of wood.

'I could squeeze in and get him,' Lucy said.

'No. I'll do it,' said her father.

But Barry said, 'I built the stack, and if anyone risks an accident in it, it had better be me.'

The woodstack was now the centre of attention. Trev, the two employees and several customers were involved in the discussions. The children waited tensely as Barry squeezed into the space where Tabby had gone. Lucy was squatting; Mark stood with bent knees and outstretched hands as if ready to catch a ball. They heard Barry muttering. Then there was a bang, a shout from Barry, and the kitten darted out, past all the waiting hands, across the yard, and hid under the Eastons' car.

'Now we've got him!' Trev exclaimed.

They surrounded the car. Around them in a larger circle were the customers and staff of the woodyard.

The children knelt down and stared under the car. Two frightened eyes stared back.

'Poor Tabby. It's mean,' said Lucy.

Their father opened the car door and took out the cardboard box they had brought with

them and placed it on the ground. He knelt beside the children.

Trev was reaching slowly towards the kitten from the other side. They saw his hand come close, closer, grab, and miss. Tabby shot out, so fast that their father missed him too. Lucy threw herself flat across the kitten's path and held him. He scratched and bit. Lucy screamed but held on. Quickly her father took the kitten from her. Trev opened the box.

The kitten went in; the lid was shut. Barry fished in a pocket and brought out sellotape to seal it down. The circle of watchers laughed and began drifting away.

Lucy's hands were scratched and bleeding.

'You were very brave,' said Mark.

'And very quick,' said her father.

Lucy felt shaky but proud.

'There's a lot of blood,' she said. 'I think I'll need a plaster.'

'Several plasters,' said her father.

Lucy nodded, pleased.

The four of them got back into the car, and Trev took the vibrating, miaowing cardboard box on to his knees.

When they got home the box was set down on the kitchen floor, next to a dish of cat food and a saucer of milk. Trev peeled off the sellotape and opened the lid.

Tabby crouched, terrified, in the bottom of the box.

'Let's all go away and let him find the food,' said Mr Easton.

The adults went into the garden, but Mark and Lucy could not bear to leave. They stood still by the back door, watching.

As soon as the room was quiet, Tabby's paws and head appeared at the edge of the box, and he sprang out. He seemed puzzled by the vinyl tiled floor, and skidded about on it. He sniffed at a chair leg, and scratched it. Then he sniffed again, delicately, appreciatively. He had smelt the food. He trotted to the dish and began to eat.

Mark and Lucy crept out and ran round the side of the house to the front garden.

Their parents and the three builders were all sitting on the lawn drinking cups of tea and talking.

Mark interrrupted: 'He's found the food!'

'That's good,' said Trev. 'He must be hungry. I wonder if he still needs his mother's milk. How long do they go on feeding them?'

'About eight weeks, isn't it?' Mrs Easton was vague.

'He isn't that old,' said Mark.

'I think he's old enough to survive without

her,' said the short fair man, who had turned out to be Dave.

'Mum,' said Mark eagerly. 'Can we keep him?'

'Can we?' Lucy begged. 'Please?'

'What about Ringtail?' their mother objected.

'I think she's forgotten him,' Mark said. 'Trev says Snowy has taken her last kitten and they all seem to have left the barn, and we don't know where they have gone.'

Trev and the other two were nodding in confirmation.

Their mother sighed. 'He's a wild cat!'

'No, he's not; wildcats are different. You only get them in Scotland now. He's a domestic cat, only he's feral.'

'Feral means wild,' said his mother. 'Look what he did to Lucy. Dave here has been telling me how hard it is to tame them. His sister used to have one and it never got really tame.'

'Of course a kitten might be easier,' said Dave.

The children seized on this. 'Can we try? Please?'

Their parents glanced at each other.

'All right,' their mother said. 'But if he can't be tamed, he'll have to go. You realise that, don't you? Like Dave said, he's probably old enough now to fend for himself.'

The children jumped about excitedly.

'We'll have to buy some more cat food,' said their mother.

'Better buy a flea spray as well,' said John, who did not seem as unfriendly as the children had feared. 'Hightop House is hopping with them.'

'Oh, great!' said Mrs Easton.

Trev laughed. 'They've latched on to John since the cats left. Seem to like him.'

John nodded. 'Right popular, I am. Flea bites all round my ankles.'

Mark was thinking about something else.

'If we've got Tabby, and the others have found a new home,' he said, 'the trapper needn't come back.'

'She'll probably come back some time,' said Trev. 'She'll need to make sure the cats have all gone if she's getting paid to get rid of them.'

'That's true,' said John. He sighed and stretched. 'Well, lads, I suppose we ought to be getting back to work.'

'It's too hot to work,' said Mrs Easton.

'Too hot to move,' John agreed. He turned to Dave and Trev. 'Tell you what: how about knocking off now and coming back about seven o'clock? It's light till ten. We could do evenings and early mornings while the weather holds.'

The three of them got up, said thanks for the tea, and wandered off, discussing the idea.

'I'm starving,' said Lucy.

Her mother looked at her watch.

'It's nearly half-past one! I'd better get you all something to eat. Oh, Lucy! Your hands! Let's see to them first. That kitten is time-consuming. I wonder what he's up to now?'

Nine Wild Cat or Pet Cat?

They found Tabby on the draining board, batting at the drips that fell from the tap.

'No!' said Mrs Easton. She picked him up. He scratched her, somersaulted out of her grasp, landed feet first on the slippery floor, skittered across it, and bumped against a broom propped up in a corner; it fell over with a crash, and he shot under the cooker and sat staring out with wide frightened eyes.

Lucy knelt down. 'Come on, Tabby. Let me stroke you.'

The kitten shrank further back. Lucy lay

flat on the floor and peered under the cooker.
'Come out,' she begged.

'Leave him, Lucy,' said their mother. 'I
want to wash your scratches.'

Lucy had lost interest in her injuries. She
got up and held out her hands absent-
mindedly to be washed, gazing over her
shoulder at the kitten, who was padding
through the open door into the living-room.
Her mother dabbed antiseptic lotion on the
scratches.

'Ouch!' said Lucy.

They heard a ripping sound from the
living-room.

Mark dashed in, followed by his mother
and Lucy.

Tabby was halfway up the floor-length
curtains, gripping with sharp claws. Mrs
Easton removed him, unhooking him claw
by claw.

Tabby sprang lightly around the room. The
television was his next interest. He jumped
up on to its slippery plastic-wood top, slid
across it and plopped into the doll's pram
which was standing next to it. There he
stayed, plucking and kneading the blankets,
turning round and round, until at last he
settled down and fell asleep.

Mrs Easton laughed, relieved. 'Let's put

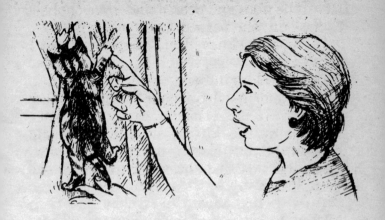

your plaster on, Lucy,' she said. 'And then perhaps we can eat before he wakes up.'

In the afternoon their father said, 'We'll go to the pet shop, if you like, and get some things.'

Mark smiled. This must mean that Tabby was staying.

His mother put a box of earth in the kitchen, and when Tabby woke she sat him on it, hoping he would understand. Tabby immediately got off and hid under the cooker.

'I'll put the doll's pram in the kitchen,' she said. 'He likes that.'

They shut him in, and drove into town, to the pet shop, where they bought cat food, a litter tray, a packet of Sani-Lit, a flea-spray, a book called *How to Care For Your New Kitten*, and a chewy plastic mouse. They arrived home to find Tabby asleep in the doll's pram. The earthbox had been used.

'You clever kitten!' said Lucy to the sleeping Tabby.

She looked at Mark, wanting him to share her pleasure, but Mark felt a strange unease. They all seemed wrong, somehow: the doll's pram, the earthbox, the plastic mouse. In the barn, with the other cats, Tabby had been learning to catch real mice. He remembered seeing Tabby stalking butterflies through the long grass in the garden; he had looked more at home there than he did now, asleep in the doll's pram. He tried to explain his feelings to Lucy, but she did not understand.

'He's funny in the doll's pram,' she said.

'He shouldn't be funny,' said Mark.

But he could not help laughing when Tabby woke and began exploring the house again. He tried to forget about Ringtail and the other cats; they were gone, and only Tabby was left, and he did so much want him for a pet.

Lucy wanted to wheel Tabby round in the pram, but whenever she moved he leapt out in terror and hid under the furniture.

'Don't do that,' said Mark. 'He won't feel

safe in it. Mum! Lucy keeps pushing Tabby in the pram and he doesn't like it!'

'He's not a doll, Lucy,' their mother remonstrated.

But Lucy still treated him as if he were, covering him with a blanket when he curled up in the pram.

The weather stayed hot all weekend. The builders came early in the morning, went home during the heat of the day, and came back at night. Mark wondered if the trapper had been back. If she had, he had not been awake late enough to see her.

On Monday the children were up early to feed Tabby. When they came into the kitchen they found the kitten by the back door, miaowing plaintively. He ignored the food Mark put out and mewed and scrabbled at the base of the door.

'He wants a wee,' said Lucy.

'No. He's used the earthbox.'

'Perhaps he just wants to go out, then.'

'We can't let him out,' said Mark. 'Not yet. We'd lose him.'

'Do you think he wants his mummy?'

'I don't know.' Mark was anxious. The kitten seemed agitated. Was Ringtail out there, calling to him? The back door glass was frosted; he couldn't see.

The kitten jumped up and tried to push the door.

'You can't go out, Tabby,' said Mark, unhappily. 'If she's not there, you'll get lost or run over.'

He was relieved when at last Tabby left the door alone and went to eat his food.

Afterwards, Mark led him by a piece of string, and the kitten leapt up and over the settee, round behind it, over the chairs, across the windowsill, until both children were shouting with laughter. Mark dropped the string into the waiting paws, and the kitten bit and clawed at it, rolling over and over on the floor.

'He likes it!' said Lucy.

Mark grinned. Tabby was happy. Surely he could not have been trying to escape?

When they came home from school Tabby was in the living-room, biting a pencil. He saw Mark and padded confidently towards him, miaowing. Mark knelt down and the kitten rubbed against him. He still cringed when Mark raised a hand, but when the hand stroked his head with one finger he purred and rose up on his hind legs, pressing against the hand.

Mark remembered how he had longed to touch the cats when they had lived in the barn, and now here was Tabby coming to him of his own free will. He pushed his doubts about keeping the kitten to the back of his mind; he wanted Tabby to be his.

On Tuesday morning when the children were off to school they saw Trev in the drive of Hightop House. They waved as they crossed the road. Trev called, 'Hang on!' and hurried towards them.

'How's the kitten?' he asked.

'All right,' said Mark.

'Great!' said Lucy

'He's getting tamer,' said Mark.

Trev nodded. 'Good. Don't know if I ought to tell you this, but . . . did you say the tabby cat with the white front was that one's mother?'

'Yes,' said Mark. 'Ringtail.'

'I thought so . . . she keeps hanging around here. She's not here all the time, but I saw her last night, and the night before. She just wanders around, making a funny little sound, not like the usual miaow. Restless, she seems.'

'Looking for Tabby,' said Mark. His spirits sank.

'That's what I wondered.'

'She wants him back,' said Mark.

'They get over it quickly, you know,' Trev

said encouragingly. 'Not like humans. But I thought I'd tell you. You'd best get off to school now, or you'll be late.'

Mark spent all day at school thinking about Ringtail, looking for her lost kitten. He couldn't bear to think that he had separated them. But when he got home Tabby seemed quite contented without his mother. And when the children fed him, although he backed away from Lucy's too eager hand, he purred and kneaded the floor contentedly as he ate.

'He's going to be tame,' said Lucy happily.

She sat on the stairs reading the cat care book, saying the words out loud and getting most of them wrong.

Mark told his parents about Ringtail. Like Trev, they said, 'Don't worry. She'll get over it.'

But Mark did worry. He thought of Ringtail searching the barn and garden, and calling for her lost kitten, and he knew he ought to give Tabby back.

Ten The Dark Garden

Mark watched his father clear the dirty dishes from the kitchen table and run hot water into the sink.

His mother and Lucy were upstairs. Tabby was asleep in the doll's pram.

His father began washing up. Mark hovered by the draining-board.

He said, 'I think we should give him back.'

His father grunted.

Mark persisted: 'Do you think so?'

'If it worries you, yes, give him back. But

she will get over it, and if you want to keep him . . .'

'I do!'

'Then keep him.'

'Supposing he never gets tame? Dave said he might not.'

'Then we'll have to let him go.'

'Would he find Ringtail?'

'Probably. But he won't need her for much longer. Cats get independent very quickly.'

Mark was silent for a moment. Then he said, 'Perhaps she won't come back tonight. Perhaps she's already given up.'

'That's quite likely.'

'If she *does* come tonight,' Mark continued, 'I think we should give him back. If she doesn't, we'll keep him.'

His father looked down, sympathetically. 'You must do what you think is right.'

'Can I go and see Trev later on and ask if she's been there?'

'Yes – but don't go making a nuisance of yourself.'

'I won't. Do you think I should tell Lucy?'

'No. She wouldn't understand.'

'Good. I didn't want to.'

Lucy was already in bed and asleep when Mark went across to Hightop House and called Trev.

'No, we haven't seen her tonight,' said Trev.

Mark's feelings must have shown in his face, because Trev grinned and said, 'With any luck she won't come. That'll let you off the hook, won't it?'

Mark nodded.

'Kittens soon grow up,' said Trev. 'She wouldn't bother about him for long.'

But another thought was troubling Mark.

'He's wild. Should he be in a house at all? A wild animal should be free.'

'Ah,' said Trev. 'Now that's a question you've got to find an answer to yourself.'

Mark went back to his own house. He ran upstairs to his bedroom and stood at the window for a while with the binoculars trained on Hightop House. There was no sign of Ringtail. His spirits rose, and yet there was guilt mixed with his relief. He had taken a wild creature and imprisoned it. Shouldn't it be free?

But I can't let him go free without Ringtail, he reasoned; he's too young to survive. The thought comforted him.

His mother opened the bedroom door.

'Come on, into bed now.'

'Ringtail hasn't come tonight. I asked Trev,' said Mark.

She smiled. 'Good. He's yours, then. Go to sleep.'

Mark put the binoculars down, drew the curtains and got into bed.

But he did not go to sleep. He wanted to stay awake until it was dark, just to be sure that Ringtail did not come. The heat and his thoughts kept him fidgeting and turning until the bed was a hot, itchy instrument of torture. He got out, found a book, and lay on top of the covers, reading. He heard the builders packing up and driving away from Hightop House. Hours later, it seemed, he heard his parents coming upstairs. He put the book away and switched off his bedroom light. When someone looked in on him, he pretended to be asleep.

Soon the house was quiet. The landing light went off. Mark got out of bed and went to the window. He crossed the fingers of his left hand. 'Don't be there,' he wished.

She was there.

The drive was empty and dark. And in the middle of the drive, a tiny lighter patch, sat Ringtail.

She's waiting, he thought. Waiting for Tabby. He thought of Tabby, as he had last seen him, curled up asleep in the doll's pram, and longed to keep him. But Ringtail was out

80

there, waiting. He knew he must give Tabby up.

He stood watching her, thinking: I can take him now. Mum and Dad might not be asleep yet. I'll ask them.

But he did not move. He stood there as the minutes went by, willing Ringtail to forget Tabby and go off to her new home.

Ringtail did not move either, and at last Mark made up his mind. He heard the sound of a car coming nearer, and as he was about to turn away from the window he saw headlights flash from under the bridge. The car slowed. The headlights swung towards Hightop House. It was the trapper's van.

As the lights sliced across the black drive, Ringtail ran. Mark saw her disappear into the shadows near the back door of the house.

The trapper! Trev had said she would be back to make sure that all the cats were cleared out. Had she seen Ringtail already? Even if she hadn't, Ringtail would soon come to her, enticed by the food in the trap. Unless he could reach her in time . . .

The landing was dark. Everyone was asleep. There was no time to wake his parents. He crept downstairs to the hall. The box in which they had brought Tabby from the woodyard was still there, next to the

81

telephone table. He picked it up, opened the kitchen door, and switched on the light.

Tabby was awake, sitting bolt upright, wide-eyed, startled by the intrusion. Mark put the box on the table. He approached Tabby slowly.

'Your mother's here, Tabby,' he said. 'She's waiting for you.'

He reached to pick Tabby up, but the kitten backed away. When Mark came nearer he hid under the doll's pram.

Be positive, Mark told himself. Like Lucy. But he was frightened of the needle-sharp teeth and claws, and once again the kitten evaded him and shot under the cooker.

Now Tabby was frightened. He would not come out. Mark thought of Ringtail, and the woman there setting up her trap, and the thought made him reckless. He lay flat on the floor, plunged his hand in under the cooker, seized the kitten and dragged him out. Tabby miaowed loudly; his claws sank into Mark's hand.

Mark ignored the kitten's struggles and thrust him mercilessly into the cardboard box and closed the lid.

The box came alive. 'Miaow! Miaow!' rose from inside. A paw broke through one corner and claws ripped at the soft cardboard. Mark pushed the paw back, but another one burst through on the other side. He felt the head pressing against the lid. He picked the box up, lodged it under his left arm, and ran to the front door.

Outside, on the pavement, with the box under his arm shifting and bumping, he stopped to make plans.

The back doors of the van were open, so the trapper was probably already in the barn. Mark did not want to risk meeting her again. And he had seen Ringtail run towards the back door of the house – her old favourite place. Perhaps she would be hiding near there.

He decided to go to the back door step. He could creep past the van and the barn door. As he crossed the road he realised that he had forgotten to put his shoes on, but it was too late to go back. He sneaked past the van. The gravel hurt his bare feet. Tabby mewed. Mark willed him to be quiet. If the woman heard . . . if she came out . . . Tabby forced his head against a corner of the box. The box was beginning to disintegrate. Despite the pain in his feet Mark clutched it tighter and ran fast up the drive and round the corner to the back door.

Ringtail was not there. He guessed she was

83

hiding in the garden or even in the woodland. If only she was not too near the barn . . .

He sat down on the door step, setting the box between his knees. Tabby was frantic, clawing at the box, thrusting out first one paw, then another. An ear and half a whiskered cheek appeared. Mark dared not let Tabby out yet in case the trapper caught him, but he wondered how much longer he would be able to hold on. Tabby miaowed loudly. The sound should bring her, if she was near.

'Miaow! Miaow!' The box vibrated. Tabby's head burst out. Mark pushed it down. The box was about to explode. Ringtail, he begged silently, please come!

But Ringtail did not come.

Perhaps the van had frightened her and she had gone far away. At least she would be safe from the trapper. But if she came back, later, and the trapper was still here, and he and the kitten were not . . . Mark knew he must try and hold the kitten until he was sure she had gone.

Tabby seemed to tire, and for a while he stopped struggling. Mark relaxed, letting his gaze wander around the garden. His eyes were growing accustomed to the dark, and the moonlight made visible familiar features: the ash tree, the boundary wall, the patch of tall stinging nettles. An owl startled him, swooping wide-winged across the garden and away into the black woodland. Mark strained to hear any sound from the barn, but there was none.

And then he saw her.

She was coming through the long grass near the ash tree, moving towards the barn.

Mark held his breath.

Ringtail came on steadily, quickening her pace. She had smelt the bait.

Mark panicked. He grabbed the box and ran towards her. Nettles stung his legs.

She heard him and stopped, startled, one paw raised. Her eyes caught the moonlight and flashed green. Mark opened the box and Tabby tumbled out.

Ringtail was already turning away. She had not seen the kitten.

'No, Ringtail!' Mark urged under his breath. 'He's here! Tabby, go to her! Start miaowing!'

But Tabby, free of the box, had nothing to miaow about, and was looking around, intrigued by the rustle of grass blades above his head.

And Ringtail had reached the broken wall of the barn.

Mark was desperate. Everything was going wrong. An idea came. He seized the kitten and thrust him back into the box. Tabby miaowed loudly in protest.

Ringtail paused. Her ears swivelled.

Mark shut the lid.

'Miaow! Miaow!' came from inside.

Ringtail turned and moved tentatively towards the sound. The mewing increased. Now Ringtail was coming fast. She knew that sound. She miaowed in reply. She had forgotten the smell of food. Her kitten was calling.

Mark opened the box. Tabby scrambled out, mewing plaintively. Ringtail was only inches away. She paused. Mark realised that she was frightened of him. He began to re-treat.

Ringtail waited until he was near the back door before cautiously approaching her kitten. Then she came forward and the two cats sniffed each other. Ringtail sat down and began to lick the kitten thoroughly all over.

Mark felt tense and impatient. What was she doing? The longer they stayed here the more danger they were in.

At last Ringtail stopped licking and stood up. To Mark's horror she began to lead Tabby towards the barn.

Mark leapt to his feet. They would both be trapped, and it was his fault! He glanced quickly around. Builder's rubble lay everywhere. He picked up a half-brick, ran towards the cats, and hurled the brick over the wall into the barn, yelling, 'No! No! Get away! You'll be killed!'

The cats fled, vanishing into the garden. Mark ran after them and flung himself down beneath the ash tree, trying to dissolve into the shadows. He knew the trapper would come out.

She did. He saw her head appear above the wall and then she climbed up. She flashed a torch here and there in the garden.

'Who's there?' she called.

She sounded scared.

Mark stayed crouched. The torchlight swung over him. His heart was thumping. The woman went back into the barn. Mark could not see the cats. He dared not leave until they were safely away.

He heard noises in the barn, bangings and scrapings, a dragging sound. What was she doing? Had she caught them after all? Was she setting up the trap somewhere else?

He heard the slam of the van doors. So she was going. He had frightened her off. The headlights came on and cut two channels through the dark. She drove the van slowly up to the house, turned round, and came down the drive. Total darkness returned as the van slipped out on to the road. The engine sound increased as it went under the bridge, then droned away into the distance.

The cats were safe. Mark felt his tension leaving him. He became aware of pain. His hands smarted; Tabby had scratched him badly. His feet were bruised and there were nettle stings all up his legs.

He was about to move when he saw them:

first Ringtail, then Tabby, emerged from amongst the dark grasses and began trotting towards the drive.

Mark got up and followed them, keeping at a discreet distance.

Ringtail moved swiftly and confidently. She ran down the drive, sprang up on to the wall, and padded along it until she came to the railway bridge. Tabby followed her as she scrambled up and over the parapet and dropped down out of sight.

Mark ran down the drive. He climbed up on to the gate post and from there on to the wall, as the cats had done. He balanced precariously along it; it was high and he felt unsure of his balance in the dark. He reached the bridge, and clambered up the metal side, pulling himself up and over the railings at the top, until he was standing on the edge of the line.

Silver rails shone in the moonlight. There were no trains. The track was empty. But further down the line, where it swung out over the water and away into the wooded gorge, he could see two small shapes moving. He felt himself to be an intruder: clumsy, cut and scratched, breathing heavily from his climb; but those two small creatures padding away from him were in their natural

89

element; they blended and became one with the night.

He watched them until their forms merged with the dark sweep of woodland. And when he could no longer see them he climbed stiffly down to the road and went home.

He had saved them, but he had lost Tabby and would never see any of the cats again.

Eleven The Secret

Mark walked slowly home from school, trailing his anorak on the ground. Lucy was not with him today. Mrs Easton had collected her at half-past three from the Infant School, but Mark had stayed on later at the Juniors' for Naturalists' Club. The pavement, usually clogged with mothers, push-chairs and dawdling toddlers, was empty.

Two lorries clattered by, and he edged in towards the trees on the other side of the pavement.

The path was slippery with fallen leaves.

He picked up a few. He was looking out for interesting things to take to the Naturalists' Club. He saw some toadstools growing in a layby where someone had parked a blue Cortina and squatted down to look at them. Better not touch. They might be poisonous. As he straightened up, a movement under the car caught his eye. A cat sneaked out and ran, belly low, into the undergrowth. A tabby with a white front.

Mark thought: it's Ringtail! He moved cautiously around the car. The cat was sitting up, looking at him. It was not Ringtail. The markings were similar to hers, but this one was smaller, younger, more jaunty . . . could it be Tabby? He stared. The cat stared back without recognition. And yet – he was almost certain now that it was Tabby.

He remembered that night when Tabby had gone back to the wild. The next Saturday his father had driven the family to the pet shop in town, and there they had chosen a kitten: a fluffy black kitten named Cinders. Cinders was tame and playful right from the start. It would have been impossible not to have loved her. She had soon made up for the loss of Tabby.

Cinders was half-grown now. Tabby would be the same, so this could be Tabby.

The cat's eyes flicked away. It got up and turned its back on him, vanishing into the undergrowth. Mark followed it. He became aware of a track, leading through the woodland. There was gravel underfoot, and, although the undergrowth crowded in, he could make out the line of an old path. He glanced back at the grassy area with the Cortina parked in it, and saw that it was not a layby at all: it had once been the entrance to a narrow country road. He pushed further in.

The remains of the path soon became thick with brambles. A steep bank rose on his right. It must be the railway embankment. The path climbed steadily upwards. There was no sign of the tabby cat. Mark pressed on, determined to see where the old road came out. His anorak was a nuisance; he tied it around his waist.

The path became so overgrown at last that he could not get through, but the top of the embankment was near. He scrambled up, hauling on a tree to drag himself out into the open and on to the railway track.

There was the cat, padding across the lines. And further on, on the far side of the lines, was a clearing with a building in it – a derelict railway station.

He had known vaguely that there used to

be a railway station in the village but hadn't thought about where it might be. This path must have been the road that once led to it.

The cat trotted along the side of the track and in through a doorway in the waiting-room.

Mark caught his breath. Could this be the cats' new home?

He came parallel with the station. Ringtail – unmistakeably Ringtail, this time – sat on a broken wall, washing her ears. Big Tom lay on a window ledge. And a black cat – Jet? – was exploring a rusty oil drum that lay on its side near by.

I've found you, Mark thought. He watched the cats, longingly, knowing it would be useless to go any nearer; they would only back away in fear. They would not remember him. They were wild.

He looked across the clearing, to the road and houses beyond. The cats were not far from human life. With a shock he recognised the flat roof of the Infant School rising above the bushes only a few hundred metres away. All this time they had been so near, and he hadn't known.

He thought of the Naturalists' Club. Part of him longed to tell them. Here were some truly wild animals, carnivores, right on their

doorstep. But he knew he would not. He would not tell anyone. Nor would he feed them, or try to come any nearer to them. They were shut away here, safe. This place would be a secret between him and the cats.

Ringtail turned her head and looked at Mark. She blinked, slowly. She didn't know him.

Mark said softly, 'Goodbye, Ringtail.'

He climbed back down to the path and went home to Cinders.